Don't Raise the Bridge, Lower the River

Rich Is Better

Help! Help! Help! Or, Atrocity Stories from All Over

The Beard

One of Our Brains Is Draining

The Yellow Submarine

A Dirty Mind Never Sleeps

My Masterpiece

The Wit and Wisdom of Hollywood

They're Playing Our Song

Memory Lane

Eliminate the Middleman

Every Day's a Matinee

The Kissinger Noodles . . . or Westward, Mr. Ho

The Golden Age of Television

The Moving Picture Boys

Get Out and Get Under

(with Audrey Wood) Represented By Audrey Wood

A Tough Act to Follow

(*with Harold Sack*) Treasure Hunt

And Did You Once See Sidney Plain?

And Did You Once See Sidney Plain?

a random
memoir
of
s.j. perelman

by Max Wilk

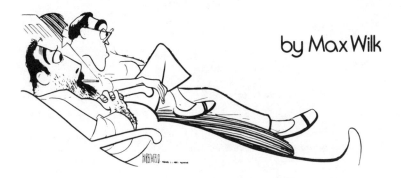

drawings by
Al Hirschfeld

W·W· NORTON & COMPANY *New York · London*

Published simultaneously in Canada by Penguin Books Canada Ltd., 2801 John Street, Markham, Ontario L3R 1B4.

Printed in the United States of America.

The text of this book is composed in 11/14 Compano, with display type set in Ronda. Composition and manufacturing by The Haddon Craftsmen, Inc.

First Edition

ISBN 0-393-02343-5

W. W. Norton & Company, Inc. 500 Fifth Avenue, New York, N. Y. 10110
W. W. Norton & Company Ltd., 37 Great Russell Street, London WC1B 3NU

1 2 3 4 5 6 7 8 9 0

Contents

CONTENTS

And Did You Once See Sidney Plain?

The Life
of the
Free-Lance

writer of humor is
highly speculative and not to be recommended as a vocation. In the
technical sense, the comic writer is a cat on a hot tin roof. His invitation
to perform is liable to wear out at any moment; he must quickly and
constantly amuse in a short span, and the first smothered yawn is a
signal to get lost. The fiction writer, in contrast, has much more
latitude. He's allowed to sideslip into exposition, to wander off into
interminable byways and browse around endlessly in his characters'
heads. The development of a comic idea has to be swift and economical;
consequently, the pieces are shorter than conventional fiction and fetch
a much smaller stipend.

—S. J. Perelman

11

Amid the Gloom of the Depression

in the early 1930s when there were soup kitchens on New York's West 40s, bread lines near Broadway, and apple vendors on each corner of Times Square, an angry young playwright named Clifford Odets exploded on that grim landscape with a stirring piece of agit-prop theatre called *Waiting for Lefty.*

On a bare and drafty stage, a company of talented actors who comprised the Group Theatre, cast as taxi drivers and their families, furiously enacted the dramatic events which led up to a dynamic climax. All evening long

13

the audience had been waiting for Lefty, a union organizer, to tell us of the state of the negotiations. Then came the shocking news: Lefty would never come. He had been found behind a car barn, a bullet in his brain, killed by those rotten finks, the tools of the greedy bosses!

"Strike, strike!" echoed through the theatre, a cry led by the angry cast, and the audience, now an integral part of the meeting, roared back, *"Yes—strike! Strike! Strike!"*

Waiting for Lefty was a violent, exciting and stunning experience. A trip to another world, indeed, for this suburban-based teenager, who had heretofore travelled through the Odetsian Bronx landscape only on commuter trains and whose prior contact with the labor movement had been the early morning "Hi, sonny" from the milkman as he lugged Borden's Grade A up the Scarsdale driveway. As I shivered in the audience, Odets' vibrant evocation of capital-versus-labor was a revelation—reality with a capital R and exclamation points to match.

Others in my class at school were rooting for the Yanks; after I saw *Lefty* I marched to the sound of a different drum. With little persuasion I might have well subscribed to *The New Masses*. From a relatively safe berth on Fenimore Road, I could have been enlisted to tramp in a White Plains picketline.

In the argot of the Party, I had been "sensitized to the endless international Marxian struggle." Who knows on which barricade I might have eventually ended had it not been for the arrival shortly thereafter of another, more lasting influence?

He was another author, a man with glasses and a trim mustache, and his connection with Marxism was not with Karl, but with Groucho, Chico, Harpo and Zeppo. I was to encounter his comedic genius in a short piece called *Waiting For Santy* (a Christmas Playlet—With a Bow to Clifford Odets), in a magazine of far higher standards than my customary reading of *Black Mask, The Open Road for Boys* and *Spicy Detective Stories.*

This brief work, my first brush with satire, took place on The Night Before Christmas, in Santa's Workshop.

(He would be S. Claus, a Manufacturer of Children's Toys, on North Pole Street, ". . . a pompous bourgeois . . . who affects a white beard and a false air of benevolence.") Within this sweatshop labored a group of gnomes named Rankin, Panken, Rivkin, Riskin, Ruskin, Briskin and Praskin, and their dialogue was a near-perfect parody of Odetsian rhetoric.

At first, I couldn't understand it. Was this author daring to make sport of my new hero, Odets, from the safety of his secure desk, in a comfortable, warm, well-furnished ivory tower? Did he not understand that the labor movement was a serious matter, that people out there, tools of the capitalist bosses (in their top hats and fur-collared coats), were starving? What did Briskin, the gnome, have in mind saying to Panken, ". . . All day long I'm painting 'Snow Queen' on these Flexible Flyers, and my little Irving lies in a cold tenement with the gout"? To which Panken would reply, ". . . You said before it was the mumps." Then Briskin, shrugging, responded, ". . . The mumps—the gout—go argue with City Hall."

Could this author be serious—daring to parody Odets? I came to the next interchange, between Panken and Briskin, as Panken passes Briskin a bowl to say, ". . . Here, have a piece of fruit."

Briskin: (chewing) "It ain't bad for wax fruit."

Panken: (with pride) "I painted it myself."

And then Briskin, rejecting the fruit: ". . . Ptoo! Slave psychology!"

I had to laugh.

At the end of the play, S. Claus gives his gnomes a forty-percent pay cut for Christmas saying, ". . . And the

first one who opens his trap—gets this." (He holds up a
tear-gas bomb and beams at them.) "We leave the gnomes
dancing for joy, all except Riskin and Briskin who ex-
change quick glances and go underground . . ."

And at that precise moment, I fell in love.

Another titan had emerged in my world, one perhaps
not so strident as Odets, but certainly one who would
prove more enduring, by name, S.J. Perelman.

We were not to meet for some time, but as years passed,
my fan-hood became fervent. Since, at a very tender age,

I had been exposed to the inner world of movie production, I soon discovered that he'd written for the Marx Brothers and done time out West on various studio lots. Those seven gnomes he had created were not only funny names with lines to match—they all existed in real life. Rankin was a legislator, Panken, a New York jurist, Rivkin was (and is) Allen, a fellow-screenwriter, as were Riskin (Robert) and Ruskin (Harry), Briskin (Sam), a producer, and Praskin (Leonard) also a scripter. The genius of this Perelman, actually only one facet of his unique gift, had been to run them all together, to re-shape them into one hilarious chorus line.

Over the Years

there would be many more such wild comedic inventions to be discovered in his oeuvre. Indeed, a lexicographer might spend the next decade in some academic hideaway, preparing *The Quintessential Dictionary of Perelmanic Names and Places.*

It would include such delightful sights and sounds as *Candide Yam,* a Chinese secretary; *Urban Sprawl,* an architect; *John Greenblatt Whittier,* poet and author of "Snowbloom"; *Pellagra & Wormser,* the biggest chain store in Richmond and *Mucho Dinero,* the Newport mansion of

HIRSCHFELD - SHANGHAI

Wolfram and Bonanza Frontispiece (their daughter was named *Wheatena*).

For those who could translate his flights of fancy from the original Yiddish, there would be, among others, *Karen Nudnic,* a choreographer, a Beverly Hills street called *North Alta Yenta Drive* and *Gaston Farblondget,* a playbroker. By far, Perelman's finest hour in this genre would come towards the close of his writing career in a piece called "Looking For Pussy," in which he recounted the story—all true— of a disastrous trip through Scotland. Miraculously, in Perelman's hands, the Highlands emerged as a Yiddish province, peopled by towns called *Milchadic, Rachmonnies, Auchundvay—Ichvasnit Grange, The Fief of Gornicht Kinhelfin, The Scourge of the Bog,* a pub called *The Star & Kreplach* and nobles dubbed *Sir Roderick de Momzer, Ivor Horseradish, The Red Chrane, Manor Sheviss, The Seat of the Homintashes,* and *Rokeach, the Thane of Nyafat.*

At the time of my seduction away from politics to humor by *Waiting for Santy,* Perelman was far from alone as a practicing satirist. There were many others who could induce laughter from printed pages; we were blessed with such talents as Robert Benchley, James Thurber, Dorothy Parker, Fred Allen, Frank Sullivan and Will Cuppy. Newspapers published Will Rogers, Kin Hubbard (doing a daily five-joke stint for years as "Abe Martin") and H. A. Smith. FPA's "The Conning Tower" featured comic verse of the highest standards. Up in Canada, there was Stephen Leacock. "He's the one who got me started," Perelman once told an interviewer. "I stole from the very best sources. I was, and still remain, a great admirer of

George Ade, who flourished in this country between 1905 and 1915, and who wrote a good many fables in slang that enjoyed a vogue in my youth. . . . and, of course, Ring Lardner, who at his best was the nonpareil; nobody in America has ever equalled him. One day, I hope, some bearded Ph.D. will get around—belatedly—to tracing the indebtedness of John O'Hara and a couple other of my colleagues to Lardner. In addition to Ade, Leacock, and

Lardner, I was also an earnest student of Benchley, Donald Odgen Stewart, and Frank Sullivan—and we mustn't forget Mencken. At the time I was being forcefully educated, in the early twenties, Mencken and Nathan had a considerable impact, and many of us undergraduates modeled our prose styles on theirs."

As the Twentieth

century moved forward, however, most of the other wits gave up on the written word. Driven to retirement by radio comedians and stand-up comics, they closed up their typewriters and moved on to other pursuits. Not so, Perelman. Right up until the end of the 1970s, he was still at it, causing one admirer to speak for all when she referred to him as ". . . a living national treasure."

For nearly half a century, starting with *Dawn Ginsbergh's Revenge* in 1929, we had those intermittent *New Yorker* pieces in which he took on any and all subjects, or per-

sons, and skewered them for all the world to see, between laughs. When he moved to Bucks County, Pennsylvania, his misadventures among R.F.D. traps for the unwary became the basis for *Acres and Pains.* When he and his great good friend Al Hirschfeld, the artist, chose to travel amid far-off lands, their overseas adventures would be celebrated with a series of brilliant bulletins, as in *Westward Ha!* and *The Swiss Family Perelman.*

But, as Perelman himself once remarked, "Comedy is a hard dollar." To increase cash flow, he contributed sketches to a revue, *Walk a Little Faster,* on Broadway in 1932 and, in collaboration with his wife, Laura, he wrote a comedy, *All Good Americans,* a year later. (He and Quentin Reynolds had also previously collaborated on a novel, *Parlor, Bedlam and Bath.*) These efforts leaked little black ink over the family ledger. So, like most of their friends, the Perelmans made periodic trips to Beverly Hills thereafter to take on such long-forgotten screen ventures as *Florida Special, Boy Trouble, Ambush* and *The Golden Fleecing.* Besides acquiring such dubious credits, Perelman stored away a large supply of venom aimed at the satraps of the studios; much of it would later seep into a comedy, *Malice in Wonderland,* which he wrote for *Omnibus,* the TV show of the 1950s.

In 1941, the Perelmans wrote a farce called *The Night before Christmas* which dealt with a batch of crooks who hide their plan to rob a bank by opening a store next to it and tunneling beneath the foundation into the vault.

It was filmed in 1942 as *Larceny, Inc.,* starring Edward G. Robinson, and every so often reappears on late-night television. By some antic stretch of coincidence, the film was run in London by the BBC, in 1971, while Perelman was residing there. A week or so later, a gang of enterprising thieves proceeded to loot a neighborhood Barclay's Bank branch of a large cache of currency, following the Perelman scenario precisely. When the press called on Perelman for his reaction, he remarked, "Maybe I ought to charge them royalties."

His first major Broadway success came in 1943; it was

the libretto for *One Touch of Venus,* which starred Mary Martin and had a lovely score by Kurt Weill with lyrics by poet Ogden Nash. A year or so later, he collaborated with his long-time friend, Al Hirschfeld, and rejoined Duke and Nash, this time on a musical show called *Futurosy.* The plot, a wildly original fantasy, dealt with the burial of a time capsule at the World's Fair. Years pass and the capsule, which contains shares in a candy company, is disinterred; the heir to the now-valuable securities is discovered to be a friendly tree-surgeon whose beat is Central Park. His misadventures as a candy tycoon in the late years of the twentieth-century may have seemed funny on script pages. The show floundered desperately in its tryout and passed quietly away in Philadelphia.

The disastrous musical was retitled *Sweet Bye and Bye,* but all that remains of it today are several lovely Duke-Nash songs which may be heard on nights when Bobby Short, in a reminiscent mood, can be persuaded to play them.

"After this disaster," remembers Hirschfeld, "we had to leave the country. Equipped with contracts from *Holiday* magazine and Simon & Schuster, we sailed around the world writing and drawing for the next nine months . . . eventually giving birth to the only book of Sid's which found itself on the 'bestseller' list. The tale of this salvation from oblivion was *Westward, Ha!*"

The flamboyant entrepreneur Mike Todd persuaded Perelman to work on the final script for his film extravaganza, *Around the World in 80 Days,* in 1956, an experience which later, as always, provided the humorist with ample material for further short pieces. Several years later, he also essayed the libretto for an original TV musical com-

edy, *Aladdin,* on CBS, which had a score (unfortunately his last) by Cole Porter.

Then came the production of Perelman's brilliant comedy, *The Beauty Part.*

In the space of two hours, he took on the entire "culture scene," aiming his slings and arrows at art, literature, film, TV—the whole ball of wax. It would star Bert Lahr, also an original talent, and the marriage of Perelman's wit with Lahr's comedic gifts was an uproarious coupling. Audiences who came were treated to a virtuoso evening by Lahr, essaying the various roles of Hyacinth Beddoes Laffoon, the editor of a smart woman's magazine; Harry

Hubris, a wily Hollywood film producer; Nelson Smedley, a right-wing Santa Barbara bigot, slightly to the right of the entire John Birch Society; Milo Leotard Allardyce Du Plessis Weatherwax, a very rich Park Avenue playboy-philanthropist, and Judge Herman J. Rinderbrust, California jurist and star of his own TV program, "The Scales of Justice."

With exquisitely bad timing, the play opened in December 1962, in the silence of the New York newspaper strike. Whatever rave notices it received could not filter through to the ticket buyers until far too late. After a brief run, *The Beauty Part* closed in March 1963 and promptly lapsed into legendary status, a collection of fond memories for those fortunate enough to have seen it and Lahr. There are Perelman fans today who, much like the characters in Ray Bradbury's *Fahrenheit 451,* can quote entire passages verbatim from Perelman's play, thus preserving great satiric literature of the past, keeping it alive and well.

Early on, Perelman

must have subscribed whole-heartedly to Somerset Maugham's rule for authors—i.e., every two years or so, pack up and move yourself somewhere else. Although for years the family home base was that farm in Erwinna, Pennsylvania, Perelman managed to peregrinate a good deal, typewriter always at the ready, across a vast global landscape. His luggage would become a mini-Rand McNally atlas of international travel, covered as it was with labels from Singapore, Bora-Bora, Bali, the P & O steamship line, Tahiti, Burma and other such exotic pitstops.

Towards the end of the turbulent 1960s, however, his wanderjahr became serious; the need for a change of scene from the American landscape urgent. Always the Anglophile, Perelman decided to try an extended stay in London. For centuries that city had always been a writer's haven. Despite the lack of a decent delicatessen—"salt beef is a poor substitute for genuine, life-giving Gaiety Deli *corned* beef," he would later complain—he persuaded his wife to pack up and try the town as a home away from home.

It was on a dark and stormy London afternoon, in No-

vember 1969, in an elegant Mayfair townhouse, recon-
verted to offices which now belonged to a film producer,
Walter Shenson (our mutual friend), that Sid and I first
became friends.

In that Green Street drawing room, high-ceilinged and
a bit drafty, where Victorian heads of government may
have plotted the course of the Empire, where Edwardian
dandies gorged and drank, Sid and I spent casual hours in
conversation. And what did we discuss? World events,
the welfare state, pollution, ecology or any such pressing
matters? No, indeed. We discussed the present state of the
moving picture business.

We reviewed a few of the more massive bank-busting
turkeys then being peddled to apathetic audiences by desperate film mavens, we gossiped about our various unem-
ployed screenwriting pals, went on to decide who was
sleeping with whom these days and then, after a decent
interval of such masochistic chat, Perelman began to rem-
inisce about his early days in Hollywood where he had
toiled as gag-man and writer.

Unfortunately, I did not have a tape recorder with me
on that long afternoon, so I must reconstruct most of our
conversation from memory. I do remember Perelman dis-
cussing a story conference he'd once had with that great
language-mauler, director Mike Curtiz (on whose set the
prop-man had once hung a sign reading, "Curtiz Spoken
Here"). We mused on certain foreign film stars imported
during the 30s, whose careers usually consisted of one
horrible film after which they were returned to sender.
Perelman's favorite failure was a long-gone Balkan
temptress named Lil Dagover, while my choice was a

male Gallic Charles Boyer clone named Fernand Gravet. How could one forget him, when the studio's own billing of his name sternly cautioned, "Pronounced Gravy"?

Sid had recently returned from Paris and a visit with his good friend Janet Flanner, the *New Yorker* correspondent there for many years. Over cocktails, the name of another European film charmer had come up, this one Jetta Goudal. The story went that she had acquired a Parisian lover, a doctor who specialized in proctology.

"Seems the lady also had a pet parrot in her boudoir," Sid reported with relish. "A bird she adored quite as much as *le docteur*. One matinee, between patients, he dropped by for a quick one, stopped by the cage to say 'Pretty Polly' and poked in his finger. The enraged bird, obviously jealous, promptly took off the tip! . . . Next week, *le docteur* changed his practice—became a dermatologist!"

We talked of various Hollywood characters and producers, such as Hunt Stromberg, an MGM titan for whom Sid had once labored. "In story conferences he paced up and down his office and dictated, not to one, but to *two* secretaries," Sid recalled. "And he punctuated the pearls he was casting by spitting rhythmically between sentences, damnedest punctuation I ever saw! We writers sat there and listened, nodding. I remember once I was in there with Dottie Parker and Alan Campbell, her husband, and we were working, or supposedly working, on a picture for Jeanette McDonald and Nelson Eddy, to be called—what else?—*Sweethearts*. Dottie sat there in an easy chair, knitting and smoking, and Stromberg kept dictating and spitting. 'I . . . see Nelson as a man-about-town,' he told us, fired with his own vision. 'Smart bachelor type

who goes to all the best places: The Colony, El Morocco, 21—very spiffy guy.' Then he turned to Dottie. 'How'm I doing so far?' he asked her. Dottie kept on knitting and smoking and smiled beatifically. 'Oh, Hunt, I do think it's *marvelous,'* she said and he beamed. He went on, dictating and spitting and then, a few minutes later, I noticed a hazy nimbus forming around Dottie's head. It was smoke! Her chair had caught fire—from her cigarette—and there she sat, totally oblivious, knitting away!"

In the ordinary course of events, when two writers have so successfully killed time, we might have proceeded to the corner local for a few pints and let it go at that, but suddenly there flashed through my head what Sam Gold-wyn is alleged to have referred to as "the mucus of an idea."

"Sid," I said, "all this stuff about your early days in Hollywood would probably make a marvelous book."

"I've already written about it," he said. "I did a piece about Irving Thalberg—'And Did You Once See Irving Plain?'—and I wrote about the Garden of Allah apartments just a couple of months back."

"Of course," I said, "but there must be a mountain of other unpublished material about Hollywood—all those stories about people who suffered and bled all those years at $1,500 a week—"

"$1,500 a week at MGM—more like $750 a week at Warner's," Sid observed, smiling. He knew my father had served out a considerable sentence as the story editor to the Warner Brothers. "But it's a good idea. Why don't you do such a book?"

"Oh no, it should be *you*," I wheedled. "You remember a lot more than *I* do."

"Wilk," he snapped, somewhat waspishly, "you are not *that* young!"

We met again, for drinks, a couple of nights later, in the tiny Mayfair mews flat he and his wife were sharing temporarily. There were more Hollywood anecdotes as we chatted and again I raised the possibility he might do a book on the subject.

Despite the instant agreement of the others present, Sid would not be tempted. There were trips he had to make, an assignment to fulfill for a travel magazine and his time was fully booked for months to come. "I've got notes for other pieces," he said, "and besides, there's that piece I'm supposed to do—needs a lot of careful research and checking—deals with a baby albino gorilla."

"Of course," I agreed. "One just can't sit down to the typewriter and write about a baby albino gorilla without being damned sure of your facts—" I stopped. "Wait a minute—*what* baby albino gorilla?"

"How many of them do you think there are?" demanded Sid. "They don't exactly grow on trees!"

It was one of the very few times I recalled his making a joke.

As time passed and we came to enjoy each other's company more often, I would learn that while this quiet, well turned-out gentleman in his sober tweeds was a good companion and a warm and friendly guest at various social events, he was never *on*.

Other gag-writers and comedy specialists I have known, most of them quite gainfully employed in films and TV, vied with each other in verbal duels and sparring matches, compulsively trying to "top" the last one-liner offered. Not Perelman. Certainly he had lines of his own, brilliant mots, to offer, but he saved them, those brilliant double or triple puns, those thrusts and parries, not for the diners asembled or for living room chat, but for the printed page. He never gave it away for temporary laughs; he consigned his jewels, thank heaven, to the permanence of linotype.

Not that his conversation lacked flashes of verbal brilliance. Sid was an avid collector of language. He picked up words or names as a beachcomber searches the sand for new shells and he would take delight in novelty. To dis-

cover that an automobile which had been badly wrecked in a crack-up was, in the parlance of the trade, "totalled," pleased him for days. That, in street Yiddish, an available female would be referred to as "a nice *zook*," was another cherished find; he would employ that word with a grin of relish. He rolled words across the tongue, savoring their essences. On a tiny alley behind Regent Street, in W. 1, could be found a small kosher dining room known as Joe Bluhm's, where displaced New Yorkers might get a necessary delicatessen fix, with properly soured pickle. Sid loved the name almost as much as he enjoyed gorging himself on that establishment's high-cholesterol viands. At 11 A.M., he might call to ask, ". . . I say, friend, would you care to join me in a bite at Joe Bloooom's, not to be confused with Bloom's?" (another famous, more imposing East End eating-hole).

At other times, he often lapsed into phraseology whose origins dated back to the 30s, when he had spent time doing comic cartoons for a long-vanished humor magazine, *Judge*. Once, in a spaghetti emporium on the Kings' Road, he was taking lunch at an all-male table. Spying two gaudy young British birds at a nearby banquette, ". . . Inhaling pasta," he remarked, he turned to one of us, a bachelor. With obvious appreciation, he suggested, ". . . Get a load of those two, will you? Why don't you go over and try some of your reliable magic on those patooties?"

By the Time of that Luncheon

it was two years since our first Green Street encounter. I had returned to America and actually managed to produce a book on Hollywood humor. Sid, having suffered greatly over the loss of his wife, Laura, had opted for a complete change of scene from his former haunts. Bag and baggage, with books and artifacts, he had departed from Bucks County, crossed the Atlantic and moved into a quiet street facing a lovely Chelsea park.

Sid had always had his loyal coterie of British fans, and, upon his arrival in London, he had promptly been taken

41

up by the establishment, both intellectual and social. He'd joined the Reform, a hospitable club in Pall Mall; he was on the very best guest lists and his morning mail was filled with social invitations TV talk show hosts wooed him for their programs; he would be bombarded daily by press interviewers who rang up requesting a chat dealing with his early days as a writer for Marx Brothers films, all of which regularly ran on the BBC. "Good God," he complained once, "All of that was forty years ago. They treat me as if I were some relic of the Neo-Plasticene era!"

But he obviously relished the adulation with which the usually reticent British showered their newly-arrived guest and, for a while, his London life was eminently salubrious. The company was good, the cuisine satisfying and most days there was a constant choice of diversions.

For London was, and is, a superb place in which to pass the time. Sans guilt, an author seeking respite from those endless solo flight hours at his typewriter can procrastinate the time away. He can stroll the streets, drop by museums or art galleries, prowl through Soho to Foyle's Bookshop, enjoy lunch with good wine and chatter, perhaps drop in at a Shaftesbury Avenue playhouse for the matinee and then proceed on to whatever home his host had suggested for drinks before tonight's dinner.

And then there was window shopping, either at department stores or side street boutiques. Every London turning leads one to new vistas and curiosities. Sid was especially fond of the small shops near the British Museum. One such establishment, over a hundred years old, featured umbrellas, walking sticks and canes of all descriptions. "Not too many places left today where a chap can pick up a sword-cane, eh?" he remarked. "Damned useful item with which to fend off footpads."

Wherever one tramped with him, he produced memories of earlier visits. One afternoon we passed by Hawes & Curtis, the shirt-makers, cheek by jowl with the Burlington Arcade, whose royal patent discreetly decorated their window, proclaiming them to be "Shirtmakers to H.R.H. The Prince of Wales of Wales."

"I was in here once with Groucho," mused Sid. "He'd bought some ties here before the war and he decided to drop in and pick up some fresh haberdashery. Inside, he asked for Mr. Hawes. The clerk said, 'Sorry, sir, but Mr. Hawes has long since retired.' 'Well, okay then, how about Mr. Curtis?' asked Groucho. 'I'll settle for him.' 'Oh, I regret to say, sir,' replied the clerk, 'that Mr. Curtis is at present deceased.' "

Another Advantage

of London living was its proximity to Europe and North Africa. Sid hit upon a proposal for travel cum pleasure, based on the famous global jaunt which Mike Todd had dramatized in *Around the World.* He offered it to his friend, Harold Evans, editor of *The Times.* It would be a modern-day journey in which Sid would emulate Phileas Fogg and recreate that character's trip, circumnavigating the globe in 80 days, wherever possible avoiding the use of air travel. If *The Times* would underwrite such a gallant venture, it would be rewarded with a series of pieces from faraway locales

in which Phileas Perelman would report back to British readers the details of his 1971 adventures. Evans promptly agreed and Sid began the preparations.

Later, it turned out he would not be going on the trip solo. A tall, blonde, young creature had read of the plan and upon meeting Sid at a party, had enthusiastically offered her services as a secretary, associate and travel companion. So insistent was she that he finally capitulated. "After all," he remarked, "she's from Arkansas and I've always had a soft spot in my heart for Southern belles."

With an ample supply of jolly-good-show and carry-on-Sid, *The Times* threw him a farewell party at the Reform on the day of his departure. Well equipped for their strenuous journey, the intrepid travelers would be taken by London cab to Waterloo Station, thence to board, in the late afternoon, the train which would take them to the Channel port, from whence they could board a steamer and brave the waters across to France. "Yes, you might indeed say we are doing this the hard way," he commented at the going-away festivities, "but I intend to remain as faithful as possible to Fogg's intrepid feat." And off went Sid and his blonde *passe-partout,* embarked on their bold adventure.

From the very beginning, the journey had far more downs than ups.

"That damned boat train was a local," Sid recounted snappishly, later. "British Rail hadn't even provided a refreshment car. We ambled on down towards the sea coast, past dinnertime, getting hungrier and thirstier by the minute, with no sustenance whatsoever save a couple of Cadbury's Fruit and Nut bars I'd brought along as a back-up *nosh.* We arrived almost an hour late, which meant we had to sprint for the Channel steamer, got aboard just in time before she sailed, to find out that its dining salon, if you could call the pigsty they provided by such a name, closed by 8:30 P.M.! With our stomachs rumbling louder than the ship's engines, we set sail, no food in sight!"

Things did not improve much from that low point. Sally Lou Claypool (the pen name he gave the tall blonde in his later articles) proved to be far from an adaptable type. Her complaints began. They were constant, loud and louder. The ill-matched pair made its way across Europe and down through Turkey and the Middle East. "With every passing kilometer, her whines continued," Sid later reported. "That girl was a natural-born shrew. She also turned out to be a female version of my own character, Nelson Smedley, the bigot. When she began

spouting loudly about white supremacy, smack in the middle of the Asiatic hordes through which we were traveling, I had the feeling I'd become shackled to a Ku Kluxer in a blonde wig!"

By the time they reached Hong Kong, Sid's patience was gone. He could no longer endure joint passage. He handed the tall blonde the balance of her ticket and requested she depart for Arkansas forthwith. Later on, Sid was to remark, ruefully, ". . . In the immortal words of the late Mayor Fiorello H. LaGuardia, 'When I make a mistake, it's a beaut.' "

Doggedly, he completed the rest of the journey alone and eighty days after his departure, he returned to London as scheduled. Nothing being so fickle as fame, Sid was no longer headline news. His arrival was barely noted by the press. And the crowning indignity was to come when he presented himself in the front hallway of the Reform, the same premises from which he had departed in such triumph months before. "Ah yes, Mr. Perelman, isn't it?" said the porter, handing him his accumulated mail. "I do believe you've been posted for non-payment of your current bill, sir."

When the articles, six short pieces in all, finally appeared a year or so later in *The Times,* they were aptly titled "Around the Bend in 80 Days." Their accumulated acerbity, not only aimed at most of the places and people he had encountered along the way but especially at the banished Sally Lou Claypool, was conspicuous. One did not need to read between Sid's expertly crafted lines, no indeed. The hostility came through loud and clear.

By that time, the gray winter of 1971–72, it was becom-

ing clear that Sid was feeling a certain disassociation with his adopted milieu. Some of the bloom was wearing off the London scene. He was moody and depressed. The British Museum *had* lost its charm. So had Joe Bluhm's salt beef . . .

Any Non Tourist

who has ever moved overseas to live in England for an extended stay can empathize with such a reaction. That first year in one's new digs, wherever it be, Mayfair, Hampstead or the suburban villages surrounding Central London, comes full of readjustments which one is cheerfully willing to make to life in a host country. If the plumbing doesn't work, if the local repairmen are fumblers, if shortages in staples occur in the shops, if department stores close for no apparent reason on Saturday at one P.M. and Harrod's endlessly bungles one's monthly statement, no matter.

Life in this foreign locale may have its little disadvantages, but novelty sustains one; grin and bear it is the daily order.

By the second winter, the euphoria sags. As the dark days drag on and the plumbing still needs repair, the transplanted begin to feel displaced. Children sulk at school restrictions and constantly refer to missed friends back home. Sinus headaches are standard equipment. Then comes Christmas. In England it is not a bit Dickensian, but rather a four-day obstacle course, celebrated by the populace in its homes, privately. Wiser heads take off for France, or Klosters. The rest of the country shuts up tight on December 23rd and remains indoors to watch the telly until the 28th.

Rare indeed is the American D.P. who can learn to live without his daily *New York Times* crossword and to make do with the Personals in *The London Times.* By February, the absence of any sunlight induces fond reveries, not of the Spanish Canaries, but of Palm Springs. Visitors from home arrive, on one-week package tours, to provide drinks at the Savoy and news bulletins, but Sunday always comes and when they've left, one is alone again. And if that BBC service does provide such quality TV, why is it so many of the British viewers prefer *M*A*S*H, Dallas* and *Kojak*? And why do the American backgrounds of those shows look better each week?

It's only if he can make it safely past that second London year that your true expatriate emerges, to put down roots. The majority of the temporaries have done their twenty-four month hitch in the British Isles and have begun yearning to give their regards to Broadway . . . in person.

So, it seemed, was Sid.

The Social Circle

which had picked him up on his arrival in S.W.3 and whirled him madly from party to party, spun on to seize new celebrities. There were far fewer affairs at which he was lionized by fans and bright young things. "Amazing how they seem to get younger all the time," he confided. "And their span of attention is so *short* . . ."

When he came to dinner, he would sit silently at the table, eating and smiling but obviously down. In drawing rooms he was a listener, rarely a participant. A trip to a distant pub to see a fabled music hall comedian, Max Wall, still at work? He would go, he would smile at the

knockabout on stage, but the audience was rowdy and unimpressed by Wall and the evening was not a success. When his turn was finished, Wall came up to the bar for a therapeutic pint and when he was introduced to Sid, he was obviously pleased. If his audience had no idea who

Sid was, Wall did. "Sorry you had to see me in this place," the comedian apologized. "The feeling is mutual," said Sid, and both men laughed.

A friend suggested a quick five-day trip to Tunisia, in January, for a change of scene. Since it was a country he'd never been to, he went along; it was one of those all-in, on-the-cheap-, off-season British holiday packages. Had he enjoyed North Africa? "Well, the price was certainly right, but you don't get too many hilarious moments out of camels," he commented.

The major problem was not diversion. It was inspiration, and he had little these days. "I can't think of anything to write about," he confided. "As much as I like London, I may have used it up. Besides, this is really not my scene."

Many times before, we had discussed the paradox of our common language: how the British and the Americans use the same words, but give them different meanings. ". . . It's their humor that confuses me," complained Sid. "It's pretty tough to get laughs out of a country where any untalented clown can break up an audience by using the word 'knickers.'"

His typewriter sat on the desk in Onslow Gardens, but most of his daily output consisted of letters. If inspiration was temporarily absent, he could find amusement in the British press. The dead-pan delivery of journalists delighted him; he cherished a clipping which reported how police had come across the body of a fully-clothed gentleman in a pin-stripe suit, in a small hillock near Land's End. The deceased's face was missing. The report ended, ". . . Foul play is suspected."

And Then There Was

L'Affaire Wigg.

It appeared that Lord Wigg, a peer of advanced age, head of the Gaming Board which supervises the operation of British racecourses, had been arrested in the West End by a London bobby. He was charged with soliciting the favors of a series of young ladies, late at night.

When hauled into Magistrate's Court, Lord Wigg had spoken in his own defense. No, insisted Lord Wigg, he had not been accosting females. In fact, in point of fact, he had merely driven his motorcar into the West End in search of a newsstand at which he might find a paper. (A fair excuse, but a bit transparent. We all knew no news-stand in London ever stays open past 7 P.M.)

After which, Lord Wigg maintained, he had driven on to discover that the antenna of his car's radio was malfunctioning. He had thereupon parked the vehicle by the curb and proceeded to raise his antenna.

"How dare they pillory this heroic man?" Sid demanded. "A sixty-eight-year-old goes out of an evening —to raise his antenna? Why, he should be put on the Honours List. Man's a national hero—a shining beacon of hope, for aging heterosexuals everywhere!"

Perhaps Wigg's misadventures might make a good humorous piece? He shook his head. "You couldn't get anybody in America to understand it," he said. "And maybe the fact that *I* think it's so funny means I've been here too long."

A New York editor had lately been in touch with Sid, suggesting he sit down and begin his autobiography. A very large advance would be paid over; all Sid had to do was sign the contracts and cash the check. He'd even come up with a title, a jewel of purest Perelman—"The Hindsight Saga."

When would he sit down and begin it?

He shook his head. "Can't do it," he said. "I've written most of my life already, don't you see? Go back and check —you've read it all, at least you maintain you have—see for yourself."

He had a point. All those years since *Dawn Ginsbergh's Revenge,* through *Keep It Crisp, Crazy Like a Fox,* and *Listen to the Mocking Bird,* to *The Rising Gorge,* his latest, he'd strewn tantalizing fragments of his career; episodes of his feckless youth in Rhode Island and at Brown; his early Manhattan days of the 20s and 30s; the Broadway obstacle course; the Hollywood squirrel cage; the disasters of country life. ". . . It's all there, don't you see?" he said. "What could I discuss I haven't already written about? Nothing left . . . and certainly not a damn thing to write about *here* . . ."

His depression was a serious matter . . . for if Sid Perelman had writer's block, than we were all in trouble.

Not long after he'd diagnosed his own ailment, he returned to the Somerset Maugham school of therapy for writers. If it involved leaving London and returning to his native haunts in Manhattan, so be it.

On the old theory that he travels fastest (and cheapest) who travels alone, he booked a ticket on the *France* for New York and embarked on a process of divestiture. He began emptying out his flat; furniture, china, hi-fi and records, all the various souvenirs and knick-knacks he'd amassed over the years. Now they were dispensible. He called in various neighborhood dealers and began to sell off items. But what was disturbing, at least to another author, was Sid's decision to sell off his library.

Brought over from Bucks Country, Sid's collection would have caused any rare book dealer to salivate. Since most of the New York and Hollywood literati had, over the years, been his friends and fans, his collection included presentation copies of first editions from Dorothy Parker, Benchley, Lillian Hellman, early Scott Fitzgerald and Hemingway. There were books of Covarrubias caricatures and Ronald Searle drawings, and since it was a working library, it was replete with old volumes he'd

picked up for research, plus the works of his early idols and influences—George Ade, Kin Hubbard ("Abe Martin"), Milt Gross ("Nize Baby") and Stephen Leacock.

A few, very few, of the rarest, he presented to close friends. As for the rest, he proceeded to call in a South Kensington dealer and requested a price for the lot. The final sum agreed upon, in her Majesty's pounds, was the equivalent of $400. That the individual books would bring a higher price for a more sophisticated buyer, or could be sent to Sotheby's, did not perturb Sid in the least. The abrupt sale was symptomatic of a sudden need to simplify his life. "I haven't the time to *hondle,*" he said, and let it go at that.

In company with another close mutual friend of Sid's, I repaired to the booksellers and without explaining why, persuaded a clerk to examine the collection, still in cartons. We bought a batch of the rarest items, to keep them safely at hand against a day when our friend might have second thoughts.

But a year or so later, when I offered them to him at home in America, he picked them up one by one, examined them sans emotion and replaced them gently on my shelf. "Very thoughtful of you, old boy," he smiled. "Glad they ended up in appreciative hands." Did he wish any of them returned? He shook his head firmly. "Let them stay here," he said. "If I need them, I can always employ you as my private librarian. I . . . ah . . . trust your daily rate is reasonable?"

Before
Sailing Home

he managed to get rid of most of his Onslow Gardens furnishings, but there arose one major problem. It spawned what we came to refer to as The Peculiar Affair of Sid's Screen.

It seemed that on his last global jaunt, he had been in a Bombay shop and what caught his eye there was a hanging screen, some six feet or so wide and six feet deep. A patient, underpaid artisan had crafted this item from woven links of plastic. Since I never actually saw it, my description must be vague. On a whim, in a rare moment of lavishness, Sid had permitted the dealer to sell it to him, on the Indian gent's firm assurance that he would ship the item to Sid, at dealer's cost.

By the time it arrived in London, Sid realized there was no room in his flat to hang it. In a large packing-case of plywood, six feet by two in dimension, it reposed in his basement storage cubicle, unopened. On the side of the case was emblazoned, in imposing letters: "TO S. J. PER-ELMAN, ESQ. FRAGILE. HANDLE WITH MUCH CARE!"

That Bombay impulse purchase would become for Sid and later, for a chain of others, an endless obligation, a Sisyphean challenge. To bring it back to America aboard ship would involve a hefty wad of francs for freight. What to do with it? The boxed item was hardly something one could toss into the dust bin. Even London trashmen could not be counted on to accept such an outsize load.

Something had to be done. Sid took steps.

"I say," he remarked to me. "Would you and your lovely frau consider taking over such an item? You'd be the first on your block to have such a conversation piece. Imagine how your neighbors would envy you."

To turn down such an exotic rarity seemed truly impolite. Sid's siren-song was an effective sales pitch. We accepted. Several days later, just before his departure, a Porsche 914, driven by our mutual pal, Eric Lister, arrived on our quiet street; jammed inside it was a strange bulky burden. Before the astonished eyes of our taciturn neighbors, the large plywood case was extricated from the sportscar, no mean feat, and carried up the steps into our rented home.

The size and shape of Sid's case must have induced gossip for days thereafter. Had those Americans down the block turned their rented home into a drop for some ring of 1972 Burke and Hare types? Were they providing corpses perhaps for Dr. J. Slattery, the medico next door?

Surrounded by his assortment of well-used gladstone bags, small trunks and fitted leather cases, Perelman was escorted to Waterloo Station and the boat train.

"Enjoy the screen in good health, bucko," he said, amid our fond farewells. "And think fondly of me as I repair to the first convenient Manhattan deli to gorge myself on pastrami, corned beef, tongue and other such goodies."

Back in New York, Sid thrived. He found a sub-lease on the Upper East Side. "Its proximity to a good delicatessen makes up somewhat for the monthly ransom charged by the gypsy queen who masquerades as my landlady," he reported. He complained about the higher cost of living, the dirt and noise and heat of a city summer, and the state of decrepit New York taxicabs. Amid the tensions, his creative juices had been restored. Contentedly, he began to write again.

The Following Spring

the Indian screen, still unopened, reposed in its bulky case in our basement. Our own stay in England was coming to an end. Now, suddenly, we were faced with the exact dilemma which had confronted Sid earlier. No steamship line would consider it personal baggage; as freight, it would cost a pretty penny indeed to have it shipped home to Connecticut.

My wife had encountered a painful orthopedic problem with a slipped disc. She lay supine in bed while our possessions were packed for the trip home. Among our needs would be another rare piece of furniture, an orthopedic chair, located with difficulty and necessary for her future. Certainly it would take precedence over a plastic screen.

What to do with that plywood box?

A rift appeared in the clouds. Since I was working on a film series for London Weekend Television, I'd become good friends with its producer, Sidney Cole. A charming chap, he'd happened to mention he was also a devoted Perelman afficionado. He lived in a quiet suburb, Ealing, in a large house. Certainly there must be space within it.

I inquired if he might care to be the custodian of a genuine Perelman item, one whose authenticity could not be questioned, not with that bold "S.J. Perelman, Esq." emblazoned on its side.

Cole was delighted with the prospect. The next day, a studio sedan arrived at our door. Once again the neighbors gaped as the plywood case disappeared into the rear seat, headed for safe harbor in Ealing.

Gone, for the nonce, but as it turned out, hardly forgotten.

It was a year or so later, during the winter, when Sid, weekending with us, casually raised the subject of the screen. "Have you opened it yet?" he inquired. "I'd certainly enjoy seeing what it looks like out of that damn crate."

I had to explain that it still remained in the British Isles, and give a thorough recital of the circumstances which had caused me to leave it behind in Ealing.

Sid nodded, impassive. ". . . Ealing?" he said at last. "Seems an unlikely repository for such an exotic item."

I pointed out that over the years, many suburban

homes had been furnished with items brought back from all over the once-vast Empire.

"Yes, but does this bird Cole have any notion what he's got stashed away?" asked Sid. "That thing happened to cost a goodly amount of my hard-earned mazumah . . ."

I assured him the screen was, chez Cole, in safe hands, that Cole was a dyed-in-the-wool fan who would never treat a genuine Perelman artifact with anything but reverence. Eventually the conversation veered on to other subjects, and I assumed the affair of the screen was closed.

My wife assured me I was wrong. "He expected it to be brought here," she insisted later. "We've rejected his beau geste. There's more to come, believe me."

Her reading of the situation was correct. A year or so later, while visiting London, I rang up Sidney Cole. According to him, he'd lately had a call from Perelman, also in London for a short stay. "He inquired about the plywood box you'd turned over to me," reported Cole, "and I, very surprised to hear from him, assured him it was safe here, and unopened as well. 'Well, I'm relieved to hear that,' he said. 'Give me directions to your place. I'm sending someone around to pick it up.' I suppose I should have been put off by that," added Cole. "I'd assumed you'd given it to me, but if he wanted it back, of course it was his. After all, I was tickled to have had a conversation with him, even such a brief one."

The next day, a car had driven up to Cole's house and Eric Lister, the same friend who'd delivered it to me, recouped Sid's plywood box.

According to later bulletins from Lister, the saga of Sid's screen was far from ended. Now that it had been retrieved, Sid had no desire to fork over inflated freight charges to guarantee its delivery back to the Gramercy Park Hotel in Manhattan, where he'd taken up permanent residence. The damned thing had become less of an artwork than a challenge, a plywood gauntlet flung. He didn't necessarily want it, but he couldn't bear losing it.

Somewhere along his daily rounds, Sid had encountered a young British actor, living in a large central London flat. Over drinks, the actor had mentioned how much spare room he had in his new abode. Sid pounced. Casually, he asked whether the actor might consider providing safe harbor for a rather unique item of property. There must have been definite echoes of Sidney Greenstreet in

The Maltese Falcon in his spiel—"Come closer, sir, and let me tell you a story about a fabulous bird . . ."

The following day, Lister delivered the unopened box to the young actor's flat. There, for the next couple of years, it reposed in a back room. Its landlord must have relished taking visitors into the rear, drinks in hand, to say, carelessly, ". . . Ah, that strange crate? It does have a story. Property of the famous writer-chap, Perelman. Left it with me for safe-keeping. See, there's his name on the side . . ."

His status as landlord to the crate was temporary. Sid had no new plans for the screen as yet, but like Wilkins Micawber, he knew something would turn up. And when it did, he would act.

Meanwhile He was Busy

He was interviewed on various TV shows, did speaking engagements at which he read from his own works, and there was an ample supply of subjects from which he could turn out several thousand well-turned words. He took various trips out of New York and found material in his travels for more pieces. Once he questioned my wife; he needed suggestions for further destinations. "But don't offer me any place that's *nice,*" he cautioned. "That's no help. What I really need is some rotten resort, or a town filled with things I can be hostile about."

One such occasion was the winter when he, in the company of his good friends Albert and Frances Hackett and Lillian Hellman, went shares on a Florida winter rental, complete with resident cook. Later, he regaled us with the horror story of that unfortunate experience.

The Florida weather had been far from balmy. There'd been high winds and on whatever pleasant days that followed, swimming on local beaches had been banned. "We were hit with something which only happens every thirty

years or so," recounted Sid. "It was obviously biding its
time, waiting for us to show up. Some infestation called
the Red Tide. Up to now I thought you only found such
an item in a Hearst headline."

There'd been indoor problems as well, specifically the
cook who'd come with the rental fee. "A demented ex-
ballet dancer—out of the closet and into the kitchen," Sid
told us. "This character kept pushing *bakerei* at us three
times daily! He wouldn't—or couldn't—make anything
but pastry! Great fat opulent iced caloric-laden land
mines, causing all to O.D. on sugar. When we complained
and begged him for some protein, he became downright
bitchy and threatened us with a knife—the same one he
used for cutting his cakes! The churl, he should have been
working for Marie Antoinette!"

As much as he enjoyed metropolitan life in his Gramercy Park Hotel quarters, wanderjahr was still the mon-
key on Sid's tweed-jacketed back. To travel was his pleasure; to have his journeys endowed the ultimate triumph.
Magazines had cheerfully underwritten his prior jaunts,
but that market had shrunk. Deep inside Sid, there was
a yen to go on one more truly splendid Big One.

He worked on it, and soon all the pieces fell into place.

It turned out that stashed away in a Bucks County barn,
the property of another kind friend, Sid had stored a
precious automotive rarity, a tiny MG, a classic British
sports car. But not just an MG, no indeed, this was a rare
four-seater he'd purchased years back on the spur of another moment. In these inflated times, that vintage vehicle
was increasing in value by the hour.

It also seemed that years ago, in the early part of this

century, the dashing Count Barzini, a sportsman, had steered an open car cross-continent from London to Peking, a truly bold undertaking in those days of non-existent roads, hostile natives and no service stations. Putting these two facts together, would it not be an exciting and fanciful project were Sid to recreate that overland run, in his restored MG, from London to Peking, with the journey itself and the rights thereto available to a publisher?

Again, his good friend, Harold Evans of *The London Times,* promptly agreed to another Perelman scheme. The notion appealed to the Englishman's sense of humor, and his financial department agreed to underwrite the trip; the good gray *Times* would be amply recompensed with a batch of vintage Perelman reports, to be written upon Sid's return from the People's Republic.

The MG was wheeled out of the barn and shipped to England, there to be overhauled and carefully restored to mint condition by the skilled craftsmen of the MG (now British Leyland) works.

Back in residence at Brown's Hotel, Sid began to cope with the trip's complex logistics . . . as well as that Bombay screen in its plywood case which, it now appeared, had once again become a problem.

That young British actor who'd cheerfully warehoused it for several years had been laid low by an ailment endemic to his profession, i.e., unemployment. He'd had to take in a paying tenant to share his rent, but his landlord had frowned on that arrangement. There was no sublet clause in the actor's lease; the landlord's solicitors were taking legal steps to regain the premises and quadruple the rent. Any day now the actor, and Sid's screen, could be out on a London street.

For almost a decade, Sid had juggled that plywood crate back and forth. What now? Certainly it could be consigned to the safety of a British warehouse, but were he to do so, it would involve paying over cash money—mazuma, gelt, spondulicks, as he referred to it. Perish forbid!

It was a challenge to his ingenuity. He'd had a good run, but it seemed that now he'd come to the end of the road . . . or had he? Should he throw in the towel, or . . . ?

In the midst of this crisis, the U.S. Cavalry appeared, riding to the rescue, this time in the person of the affluent American gent who'd bought Sid's farm in Bucks County. In company with his fiancee, a most attractive lady, the gentleman had arrived in London and promptly invited Sid to a celebratory dinner at a smart, over-priced restaurant.

Midway through the festivities, Sid played his trump card. "I would like to present you two lovebirds with a wedding present," he announced. "It's a very rare item I picked up on one of my trips to India—a screen, cunningly crafted by some Indian artisan. I can just imagine it now, hanging in your Erwinna bridal bower, swaying softly back and forth. Would you accept it from me?"

Who could resist such a lavish offer?

Ah . . . but there was still a tiny logistic problem. Said screen was here in London, and Sid was obviously too busy here to present it properly to them in far-off Pennsylvania.

No matter. His American friend would be delighted to cope with the problem. He would underwrite the screen's transport to America—by air freight, yet!

Done, and done. Out of the teeth of disaster, Sid had

snatched success. Within hours, the plywood case was retrieved from its shaky repository, once again by Eric Lister, who delivered it to the grateful couple's hotel. The following day, a decade after it had arrived in London, the screen was finally on its way to America!

Upon his return to Manhattan, just before departing on his London-Peking run in the restored MG, Sid provided the final (or next-to-final, as it turned out) bulletin on the screen's progress. 'The happy couple has made it legal," he reported. "They invited me down for the weekend. I was escorted into their master bedroom and there, properly hung, swaying in the gentle breeze above the connubial playground, was the screen."

After all those years in storage, hidden away, how did that six-foot Bombay souvenir look?

Sid shrugged. "Actually, I found it a little ostentatious. Nothing *I'd* want to give house space to. But I'm glad I found it a good home," he added, pointedly.

In 1978 He Embarked

on that London-
Peking trip. A backup for his tiny MG, a reliable Land
Rover, had been arranged and two others joined him for
the trek; one was his old friend Eric Lister, the other a
driver-mechanic from the MG works.

What had been planned as a pleasant jaunt soon
degenerated into a daily endurance contest. Their long
and arduous journey was an obstacle course, not much
better than Barzini's original run. Bad roads, even worse
weather, sketchy accommodations and rotten food . . . the
trio encountered them all.

They made it safely to Hong Kong, but the People's Republic of China seemed unimpressed by the whimsy of a bespectacled gent in a vintage MG who requested permission to drive down the main boulevards of Peking. He could come to Peking as a visitor, alone, but sans car; no amount of argument at the Chinese legation could persuade the officials to change their minds.

Sid went on alone, by train, to Peking.

There he was promptly felled by one of the infectious viruses which populate the People's Republic. He developed pneumonia and was taken to a Chinese hospital. Once the doctors had restored his health, he left, headed for the Gramercy Park Hotel . . . and a decent meal in a delicatessen.

There
Would Be

no further travels, and there are, alas, no articles extant which document that final journey. No typical Perelman diatribes against the disarray, stupidity and pot-holes which punctuated his expedition in the MG. *The Times* was undergoing a near-fatal strike in London and had shut down. Had Sid written the pieces, they'd have waited, unset in type, until publication began once more. So *The Times'* loss is our loss.

Ah, well, tant pis (or better still, *nitgedaigit* . . . not to worry), we can count our blessings. Happily for us, there

are all those books of his on the shelves, for future generations to discover and cherish.

A half-century of the visions of Sidney Joseph Perelman, a traveler in his own special world, peopled with world-weary playboy Poultney Groin, Basil Clingstone, the actor (last seen locally as the Second Sculptor in *Father Praxiteles' Chickens*), Downey Couch, the Irish tenor and his friend Frank Falcovsky, the Jewish prowler. Establishments such as Le Gangster, Beverly Hills' ranking French restaurant where dines Monroe Sweetmeat, the head of Subcutaneous Pictures, in company with lovely Fern Replevin (an utterly lovely creature of 24, whose mouth wanders at will over her features). Steamships known as the S.S. Choleria, which will possibly take Gossip Gabrilowitsch, the Polish pianist, to Europe where, in Paris, he can check into the Hotel of the Cheap Valise, in Montmartre, in company with Sir Joseph Mushroom, for whom that growing plant was named . . . and on, and on . . .

And for those of us fortunate enough to have coffee-housed, wandered the streets, exchanged pleasantries or enjoyed hot pastrami, a cream cheese and Nova on a bagel or, in desperate circumstances, a salt beef at Joe Bloooom's with the master, we have fond memories (as well as the echo of Heartburn Past) to sustain us.

Oh yes, about that Bombay screen. According to latest reports, the Bucks County marriage, after a brief run on the double bed, came apart at the seams. The once happy couple have split . . . pfft . . . packed it in.

Who got custody of Sid's plastic screen? After its ten years of wandering, where is it now? It seems to have vanished from sight . . . truly a case for Scotland Yard, eh, inspector?

At the very least, it should be hanging in some good delicatessen, swinging gently to and fro amid the corned-beef laden breezes.

It May
Surprise You

to hear me say—
and I'll thank you not to confuse me with masters of the paradox like
Oscar Wilde and G. K. Chesterton—that I regard my comic writing
as serious. For the past thirty-four years, I have been approached almost
hourly by damp people with foreheads like Rocky Ford melons who urge
me to knock off my frivolous career and get started on that novel I'm
burning to write. I have no earthly intention of doing any such thing.
I don't believe in the importance of scale; to me the muralist is no more
valid than the minature painter. In this very large country, where size
is all and where Thomas Wolfe outranks Robert Benchley, I am content
to stitch away at my embroidery hoop. I think the form I work can have
its own distinction, and I would like to surpass what I have done in
it.

—S. J. Perelman

The Author

Max Wilk's friendship with S. J. Perelman began in 1969 while both were writing and living in London. Wilk's novel, *Get Out and Get Under* (Norton), is a story of classic car buffs, another interest the two humorists shared. Wilk has written for American and British television and films, put together an anthology of Hollywood humor, and authored a dozen novels and biographies. His latest, *A Tough Act to Follow,* is set in the early days of "live" television, of which he is a veteran.

The Illustrator

Al Hirschfeld was one of Perelman's dearest friends and a favorite collaborator. Though world-famous for his theatrical drawings, some of the artist's finest work was done when he was collaborating on books with Perelman. Shortly after World War II Hirschfeld and Perelman set off on cruises (sponsored by Simon & Schuster and *Holiday* magazine) that resulted in the delightful *Westward Ha!* and *The Swiss Family Perelman.* The Hirschfeld drawings here were originally published in *The London Times, The New York Times,* and *Holiday.*